Rebound

A Tryst Island Erotic Romance

SABRINA YORK

DEDICATION

This book is dedicated to Carrie Jackson and Alexandra Cross. When you read the book, you'll know why, if you don't already.

ACKNOWLEDGMENTS

First of all, thanks to my amazing beta readers, Sherene Kershner, Charmaine Arredondo, Ronlyn Howe, Kathy Klein & Monica Britt. My deepest appreciation to Wicked Smart Designs for a rocking cover, and to Marie Force and her Formatting Fairies for helping me whip this novella into shape.

Over the past year I have enjoyed the support of some truly amazing fellow authors and bloggers, without whom I would be languishing in a padded room. I love them all, and so appreciate their support and friendship. Please pick up their books if you're in the mood for some really sexy, spicy, fun romantic fiction, or visit their blog pages: Desiree Holt, Chantilly White, Cassiel Knight, Cathy Brockman, Cerise de Land, Cindy Spencer Pape, Cristal Rider, Danita Minnis, Delilah Devlin, Emily Cale, Frances Stockton, Jianne Carlo, Kate Hill, Kendra Edens, Lisa Fox, Lissa Matthews, Mel Schroeder, NJ Walters, Paloma Beck, Sidney Bristol, Susana Ellis and Tina Donahue.

To all my friends in the Greater Seattle Romance Writers of America, Passionate Ink and Rose City Romance Writers groups, thank you for all your support and encouragement.

CHAPTER ONE

Kristi Cross set her heavy suitcase on the deck encircling the house and stared at the last trails of sunset shafting through the clouds and dancing on the darkening water of the horizon. She stilled, captured by the beauty, the peace, the perfection of the moment. She loved living in the Pacific Northwest, and this was why.

It had been a long, frustrating day. She'd planned to spend it puttering in her shop, closing at four and heading out to the island for a weekend with friends. But no. Instead she'd wasted hours attempting to converse rationally with a city zoning-bot who wanted to make her funky, friendly neighborhood into an industrial complex. And then she'd endured more aggravation at the DMV trying to explain she was, in fact, who she was. And of course there was that trial of patience at the post office, standing behind a very charming elderly woman who insisted on paying for everything with pennies.

Which she counted out. One. At. A. Time.

But this? This panoply? This glorious splay of color and nature and peace?

It made it all worth it.

She was ready for a break from real life, thank you very much.

And it had nothing to do with that nasty scene with Rolf this morning.

Truly. It didn't.

Besides, that relationship had been over long before she'd walked in on him fucking her best waitress in the storage room.

There was no other word for what she'd witnessed. Fucking. Plain and simple.

No doubt, she'd miss Savannah more than Rolf. He hadn't exactly been present, only paying attention to her when he wanted sex. She should have dumped him months ago.

1

It was a pain in the ass being in a relationship all by yourself.

The last gasp of sunlight winked out, and a velvet blanket draped itself over the horizon. Kristi couldn't see it, but she could hear it, *smell* the sea. Her soul knew it was out there, vast and beautiful, constant and soothing. And that was enough.

With a sigh, she picked up her suitcase and let herself into the back hallway of the vacation house she shared with a group of college buddies on an island nestled in Washington State's San Juan archipelago. The island's official name was Trystacomseh, after a long-dead Indian chief, but the locals called it Tryst Island for short. She didn't get out here very often because her business, Beanie's Book and Coffee, kept her tied to the counter. But after a day like today, she really needed it. She'd checked the online calendar and been ecstatic to find a spot open—this was a last-minute whim, and the house was completely booked on many weekends. There were only so many beds, after all. Lucy had agreed to cover her Saturday shift, so Kristi had packed a bag and headed over to the ferry terminal.

Because her day was going the way it was, she'd missed the ferry. But she'd been able to catch a ride with Darby Britt, who'd been in Seattle stocking up on supplies for the bar.

In a perfect world, she would never have climbed into a boat with Darby. He drove like a demon escaping hell. But she'd needed the ride. And frankly, she'd enjoyed the feel of the wind whipping past, the tang of the sea spray and the sense she was jetting far and fast from the annoyances of her life.

Her hair would probably never be the same.

She smoothed the tangled locks into what she hoped resembled a human configuration as she checked the white board on the wall by the back door, just to see who had signed in—and her pulse stalled.

Damn. Of course *he'd* have to be here. What were the odds?

Kristi had had a mad crush on Cameron Jackson since her freshman year in college. Everything about him had drawn her, from his tall muscular form to the broad, friendly smile. He had a wicked sense of humor and could keep up with her snarky banter.

Of all the Dawgs, as they called themselves—the eleven souls who'd lived in McCarty Hall at the University of Washington and formed a bond while screaming at the television during football season—Cam was, by far, the most gorgeous. For four years, when they'd all converged on the lounge for their gridiron fix, she'd lusted after him. Even knowing—*knowing*—she wasn't his type. Not by a long shot.

She'd lusted after him when they weren't watching football too.

And damn it, she still had that stupid crush on him.

It was stupid. Really it was.

Kristi nibbled her lip. "You could have asked me how crazy-making she was."

He barked a laugh.

"Or you could have asked Jamie. Or Cassie or Emily or Kaitlin. Or Lucy. Especially Lucy."

"Seriously?" He gaped at her. "No one liked her?"

"None of the girls." She shot him a saccharine smile. "I'm sure the guys appreciated you bringing her around. Especially when she wore that floss thingy. What do you call that again?"

"A bikini."

"Was it? Was it really? Because I think they cheated her. Or she forgot to put it all on. Or—"

"Now Kris. Your claws are coming out."

"It could at least have covered her butt crack. Nevertheless," she smirked, "the guys liked the view."

"Well they can have her." Something must have flickered over her face. His eyes narrowed on her. "What?"

"Nothing."

"Aw Christ. Did she make a play for one of the guys?"

She didn't answer. She couldn't. Instead, she said, "Would you really wish her on your best friends?"

"Hell no. The last thing I want is to see her again...especially here."

Kristi twisted her napkin. That would be...awkward. "Well, anyway. I'm sorry about all that, Cam. I know how it feels to walk in on someone you..." She trailed off and frowned at her beer. Somehow the bottle was empty. "I'm getting another. You want one?"

"Sure."

He watched her head back to the kitchen—she felt the heat of his stare all the way to her core. Like he had some kind of laser vision.

Again, probably her imagination.

She did have a very active imagination.

At least when it came to Cam Jackson.

As she handed him his beer, their fingers brushed. She was able to hide her visceral response to his touch, but he probably didn't miss the flinch.

He cleared his throat. "So... You've walked in on someone?"

"What?" She'd lost the thread of the conversation.

"You said you know how it feels."

"Ah yes." She plucked at the label on her bottle. Just to have something to distract her. From him. "Same dealio with Rolf."

"Really?"

"Hmm." She gazed out the wall of windows at the ocean in the distance, but it was dark, so all she could see was their reflection in it. Her attention naturally gravitated to him. She could tell he was studying her intently. She had no idea why.

"Want to talk about it?"

"Not really. We're done, he and I." He chuckled and her head snapped around. "What's so funny?"

He winked at her. "I never liked Rolf either. I thought he was a douche."

"He is."

"And why does he think he's God's gift to women? Prancing around like he owned the place? Making those idiotic, cocky comments—"

"He thought he was clever."

"That's what you get for thinking."

Kristi couldn't hold back her snort. She grabbed a napkin as beer shot out her nose. Cam could always make her laugh, even when life wasn't very funny.

He crooked a brow and smiled wickedly. "Need another beer?"

She chuckled. "I better not."

"Wanna play Hearts?"

Kristi checked the clock. It was just eight. They had at least a couple hours before everyone came back from the bar. And she did love a good game of Hearts. "Sure."

He nodded and dealt the cards. They were halfway through the first hand when he broke the silence.

"Do you remember the first time we played?"

"You had to teach me."

"Took me all night."

"That was hardly my fault." She rearranged her cards. "You kept pouring me shots."

"You're the one who kept drinking them."

She feigned a pout. "I had to keep up with Jamie."

"Now, *she* was easy to beat."

"So was I, once you got me liquored up."

His chortle rumbled through her. "You figured out my strategy." He shot her a saucy leer. "You sure you don't want another beer?"

"No way. I'm winning this game, buster."

They played for a while longer before he spoke again. This time, his words sent a scalding sizzle through her solar plexus. "You know Kristi, I can't remember a time when we were both…single."

Her heart seized. "*What?*" Thank God she hadn't just taken a sip of beer—she would have spewed it across the table for sure.

"Think about it. Since the day we met, one of us was always in a relationship."

Usually him.

She didn't respond. She didn't know what to say.

8

And she wasn't with Rolf.

And, win or lose this game, he was going to win. He was going to get what he wanted. He was finally—*finally*—going to taste her. Maybe more. If he was lucky. He hoped to hell the others stayed at the bar long enough for his plan to come to fruition.

Though it wouldn't hurt to speed things up and throw the game.

He tossed out a card.

She wrinkled her nose—damn, she was cute when she wrinkled her nose. "Really, Cam?"

"Huh? What?"

"That's your lead? The queen of spades?"

"Yup."

"Are you trying to shoot the moon? Because I already took a point."

"Just play." She shook her head and underplayed the queen. He ate a whopping thirteen points. And then he led with the jack of diamonds. She took it with her ace and then went on to win the hand.

He really wasn't paying attention. He was busy planning his assault. If he lost the game, *he* got to kiss *her*. And he wanted to *kiss her*. In fact, the desire, the need to orchestrate the entire clinch bubbled deep in his gut.

He dealt again, trying not to glance at the clock. This should be the last hand if he played his cards right. Or wrong, as the case may be.

And yes. She won. Easily. In fact, she spanked him.

Although he didn't let his mind linger on that image. It was far too distracting.

Instead, he leaped to his feet so quickly his chair toppled over. He ignored it—and her little *'eep'*—and came around the table in a rush to yank her into his arms and…yes! Yes. The feel of her, molded against him, was delicious. He'd known it would be.

The scent of her shampoo, or her perfume, or just Kristi, enticed him. He drew it in, savoring the moment, the knife's edge of intense anticipation.

"You won," he murmured, gazing down into her wide hazel eyes. "Now I have to kiss you."

Her lashes fluttered. Her lips pursed. She wiggled a little against him and his cock stirred. "You *have* to? Well, isn't that just—"

She didn't finish. Whatever she'd been about to say never made it out of her mouth because he took her then. He dipped his head and settled his lips over hers and ate the words, consumed them. A thrill shot through his solar plexus at the contact. Warm, supple, sweet. Fragrant.

He surprised her by diving in like that. She went a little stiff, but it didn't take long for her to relax and respond.

And hell. Did she respond. Did she ever.

The kiss, which he'd intended to be slow and provocative, quickly raged into something else altogether. And when she uttered a throaty moan and her tongue peeped out to touch his, he nearly lost his mind.

He changed the angle of his head and deepened the kiss, holding her in place with one hand to her chin. The other roved.

God, she was amazing. He drew his palm over the flare of her hips. It dipped in at her waist and then rose up her ribcage. He nearly passed out when he skimmed the underside of her breast. Nearly passed out because all the blood in his brain shot straight to his cock. His whole body thrummed with every beat of his heart.

He cupped her and she made another charming little noise. When he scraped a thumb over her nipple, she whimpered.

He longed to suck it. Draw it into his mouth and nibble and nip. Make her thrash.

He lifted her up onto the table and when she started to protest, he shifted his attention to her neck, nuzzling her there, right behind her earlobe. She gasped and garbled a word that might have been "more" and dug her nails into his shoulders.

He loved that as he drew her higher, teased her to a fever pitch, her responses became like his—feral.

He'd known she'd be like this in her passion. Wild. Unrestrained. Demanding. He loved it. Fucking loved it…but he wanted, needed, more.

He fumbled with the buttons on her blouse.

His euphoria tumbled into the dark abyss when she stopped him. He pulled back to look at her, although pulling back was the last damned thing he wanted right now. Fortunately, a tiny chunk of his brain was still functioning. It reminded him he'd been raised to be a gentleman.

He could go for the jugular again. He could renew his attack on the sensitive spot he'd found, the one at the base of her neck that made her warble and squirm and arch into his cock with a mind-bending pressure. He could make her forget whatever stupid objection she was about to present.

But he wanted more than a mindless fuck with Kristi.

He wanted a lot more.

"What is it?" he asked. And damn, his voice was rough. He barely got the words out.

"You–you said one kiss."

"I wasn't done yet."

She laughed as she pushed him away and rose from where he'd splayed her on the table.

Yeah. He'd been ready—he was ready—to fuck her on the dining room table.

Some evil ifrit in his head howled at the idea of all the future meals they'd share. Here. At this table. And none of the other Dawgs would know the manner in which he and Kristi had defiled it.

Lucy would fucking kill him if he screwed her business partner—or

Drew snorted. "I wish. At least fighting a fire is exciting. This week we broke in a new recruit. I swear. I don't know where they dig up some of these guys."

Lane clapped him on the shoulder. "Ah, the younger generation."

"Shut the fuck up, you ass. We're hardly geezers."

"Aren't we? It's not ten o'clock and we're all going to bed. On a Friday night." Lane quirked a brow and headed for his room, the only one on the main floor. "Night y'all."

"Night," everyone chorused.

While they were all focused on Lane, Cam leaned in and whispered, "Come to my room tonight."

Kristi blanched. "I can't!" she burbled. "Cassie and Bella will find out."

"Wait 'til they fall asleep. Come on, Kristi. Don't leave me like this." He pressed her hand against his erection and surged into her for good measure.

She smirked. "You started it. What were you thinking, teasing me like that? That I'd just sit back and take it?"

"The thought crossed my mind."

She pursed her lips and repeated his snarky words from earlier. "Well, that's what you get for thinking."

He hooted with laughter. He was about to respond when Holt, who'd been heading for the stairs, called back, "Aren't you coming, Kristi?"

Cam's teeth came together with an audible click.

"In a minute," she said and then, just to placate Cam, who looked like he was about to pop a gasket, she added, in an undertone, "I'll try to come."

"Try hard," he growled.

She shot him an impish grin. "You can play with yourself while you wait."

Judging from his glower, he didn't appreciate the suggestion in the slightest.

CHAPTER FOUR

It took Cassie and Bella forever to fall asleep.

Just when Kristi thought they'd dropped off, one of them would say something and the other would respond and a muted, sincere conversation would ensue—despite Kristi's deliberate snoring.

How rude of them.

Chattering away as though someone in the next bed wasn't trying very hard to pretend to be asleep.

They finally drifted into silence. Kristi strained to listen to their breathing, only stirring when she was certain they were asleep. She eased off her covers and tiptoed from the room, glad she'd brought her full-length nightie so she didn't have to flit through the house in her teddy. Although Cam might have enjoyed that.

Of course, when she packed, she had no idea she'd be plotting an illicit tryst. Or she might have tossed the teddy in.

It seemed like every stair creaked as she made her way down to the great room. She winced with each step. The room was dark, cloaked in shadows. While she did enjoy the stillness of the night, she didn't appreciate stubbing her toe on the coffee table. Thankfully she thought to muffle her curse.

Her yelp—when a dark form stirred and rose from one of the easy chairs—was a different matter entirely.

Holt's low chuckle resonated through her.

"Shit, Holt. You scared me to death."

"I was wondering when you'd come down."

She frowned at him through the gloom. "What made you think I'd come down?"

He stepped closer. "I'm not blind."

"Blind?"

"Yeah, I saw what was going on between you and Cam. I figured you'd make your way to his room sometime."

"And you waited up—why?"

"Isn't it obvious?"

"No." It was annoying. That's what it was. All she wanted was to continue her journey into the bowels of the house and slip into the bed of the man who was waiting for her. And hard for her. And—

"I meant what I said, Kristi. About choosing. But in order to choose, a woman has to know she has a choice."

"What are you talking about?"

"Us." The clouds broke just then and a faint shaft of moonlight sighed into the room. The look on his face was alarming. *Hungry.*

Her mouth went dry. "Holt, there is no us."

"There could be. God damn it, if I'd known you were coming this weekend, that you'd finally given that smarmy ass his walking papers, I'd have been here waiting for you. Instead, Cam got the opening I've been hoping for."

She shook her head. "No, Holt."

"No, what?"

"Just no. It's always been Cam for me. Always. Ever since...well, always." She set her hand on his arm, just to comfort him.

Big mistake.

He caught her wrist in a tight cuff and yanked her against him. He was big and strong and held her in a vise. "Maybe this will change your mind."

His mouth settled on hers, hard and demanding.

If she'd been any other woman, she would have been moved. She would have been seduced. He knew what he was doing and kissed like the very devil.

But he wasn't Cam.

She let him finish, just so he could tell himself he'd tried. But she didn't respond. Sometimes apathy spoke more powerfully than resistance. When he lifted his head with a hopeful expression she smiled. Sadly. "Nope."

"Shit Kristi...that was a damn good kiss."

"It was very pleasant."

"Pleasant?" he squawked.

She shrugged. "Sorry, buddy." She probably shouldn't have emphasized the word, but she needed to make a point.

Clearly, he missed it.

"Okay then. How about this?" He kissed her again, this time with a tinge of desperation. He nearly suffocated her with his presence, pressing into her and clutching her and working her lips.

He kissed her and kissed her and kissed her. And he didn't seem inclined to stop anytime soon.

Kristi forbore tapping her toes, but she was getting a little impatient.

What she wanted—all she wanted—was to be with Cam. After a while, she tried to gently disengage, but he wouldn't release her. She was on the verge of wracking him in the balls, which she really hated to do to a friend, when she was ripped from his arms and flung across the room. She landed with an *"oof"* on the leather sofa.

A sharp crack resounded, along with a feral growl. Something that sounded like, *"Mine."*

Holt reeled back and collapsed in the lounger.

Cam turned to her with a ferocious glower and whipped her into his arms. His body hummed with tight tension. She suspected he would have tossed her over his shoulder if he'd needed to.

He didn't need to.

She was right where she wanted to be.

He'd lifted her so effortlessly, it made her feel like a delicate china doll. She wrapped her arms around his neck and snuggled closer as he carried her down to the basement. She loved that he'd stormed to her rescue wearing only his pajama bottoms. His chest was bare and broad and warm.

"My hero," she whispered into his ear, and he relaxed, but just a bit.

"I was wondering what was taking you so long."

"Bella kept chatting."

"Bella's a chatterbox. She needs a man to take her in hand."

"Mmm. I like the sound of that." She toyed with his nipple. He nearly missed a step so she decided not to do any more of that until they were finished with the stairs. "Would you like to take me in hand?"

"I'd like to turn you over my knee."

She chuckled. "Me? What did I do?"

He gaped at her. "Other than passionately kissing Holt?"

"I wasn't kissing Holt, and you know it."

"Really?" He crossed the rumpus room and shouldered into his bedroom and tossed her onto the bed. She bounced. "Then what the hell was that?" He waved at the ceiling.

Kristi straightened her nightgown, primly covering her bare calves. *"He* was kissing *me."*

His brows bunched. "Not okay. Do you know what seeing that did to me? God, Kristi. It ripped me up inside. I wanted to *kill* him."

"He had to know."

"Know?" He hit a warbling tone that would make America Idol contestants green with envy. "What did he have to know?"

"That I feel nothing for him."

That shut him up. He stopped, stock-still and stared at her. "Nothing?" This, in a little boy voice.

Other than shock that two of her longtime friends had declared their intentions in the space of one evening? "Not a thing." She wormed her way off the bed and sashayed toward him, swinging her hips. "Less than nothing, in fact." She stood on tiptoe to press a kiss on his lips. "It was like kissing my brother. Or my uncle. Or Professor Layhea."

"Professor Layhea?" Against his will, his lips tweaked. She could tell he was fighting it. His pout was kind of adorable. "Professor Layhea *was* pretty sexy."

She kissed him again. Made her way along the line of his jaw to his lobe. Dabbed her tongue in his ear. He shuddered.

"I do find nostril-beards *über* sexy. And older men who take their baths in Old Spice—ha cha cha."

His brow rose. His fingers curved around her waist and he pulled her closer. His cock stirred against her belly. "Did you ever kiss Professor Layhea?"

"Just the once." She laughed when his eyes boggled at her boldfaced lie. She rubbed against his growing ardor. "I had to. I needed an A."

"Hussy." He eased her back onto the mattress pinning her there with his hardness, his heat. He hovered over her, staring at her for a long while. Then he slowly lowered his head and kissed her.

It didn't take long for their teasing mood to completely evaporate. It was replaced by a crackling arousal. His cock pressed into her with an uncomfortable insistence. She wiggled a little bit and he shifted so it pressed against her cleft instead. He rubbed, up and down, like a cat, until she moaned.

"I shouldn't want you again," he murmured against her lips.

"Of course you should."

"You drained me completely fucking dry earlier."

"We forgot to use a condom."

He nibbled her neck. "You're on the pill."

She hiked up her nightgown, enough so she could hook her legs around his butt. Tugged him closer. "I can't believe how many times you made me come."

"How many?"

"I lost count."

"Really? I noticed two."

"Oh, there were more than two." She scored his back with her nails; he shivered. "It was probably a fluke though."

He reared back. "What?"

"You know. On account of the fact I was so horny."

"How, um, how horny were you?"

"Pretty horny."

"How long… I mean, how long since—"

She drew his head back down. "I don't want to talk about it. Point is, it was probably a fluke."

"It wasn't a fluke. I'll have you know, I'm damn good in bed."

"We'll see."

"What? *We'll see?*"

"We haven't done it in a bed." This, she stated rather prosaically. "We'll just see if you can do it again. Make me come like that again."

A slow smile quirked his lips. "That sounds like a challenge."

"I do believe it was."

"Well, madam, if there's one thing Cameron Jackson cannot do, it's resist a challenge." He teased her hem higher and she laughed.

"Yes," she said. "I know."

Funny.

Funny and sexy and damn stimulating.

That's what Kristi was.

Perfect.

She even wiggled out of that prissy nightgown when he rolled to the side, pulling it over her head and tossing it over his shoulder. His breath caught in his throat as her breasts bobbed free. Glorious.

"Well," she said with a tiny frown. "What are you waiting for?"

"I'm not waiting. I'm savoring." He cupped her firm full mounds. Their weight delighted him. Her nipples perked up, even as he stared at them. He couldn't resist drawing one, then the other, into his mouth. Delicious.

She squirmed at that, rubbing against his cock.

He pressed her breasts together and did what he'd been yearning to do since he'd seen her in her swimsuit last summer, buried his face between them and drew in her scent. Exquisite. She smelled like summer. Like summer and talcum and woman. A groan hovered at the base of his throat. She was so soft, so pliant. Everything about her was welcoming.

"Hey, mister," she muttered. "You're not pleasing me. You're pleasing yourself."

He chuckled and lifted his head. "Oh, I'll please you. I'll have you screaming for mercy in a minute."

"You wish."

"*You* wish."

"I guess my challenge wasn't challenging enough."

He scooted up, until they were nose to nose, tunneled his fingers through her lush brown hair and held her still as he kissed her. Kissed her as though his life depended upon it. Which he suspected, in one tiny corner of his soul, it did.

He could kiss her forever, he thought. He could nestle in and lap and lick and suckle those lush pink lips. He could crawl inside and explore with his tongue and nibble and nip until eternity came knocking on the door.

His cock had other ideas.

As he seduced her, coaxed her, cajoled her with his mouth, the monster rose, until he was so hard and full he ached. The only way to assuage the nagging hunger was to press against her. Even that wasn't enough.

He wanted to pull down his pajama bottoms and slip into her creamy depths. But she'd issued a challenge. And he was determined to answer it. He wanted to make her come. Make her so crazy for him she'd beg, plead, howl to be fucked.

He could think of a couple ways to accomplish that. He decided to go for out and out teasing. Slowly, he made his way over her chin to her neck, feasting there until she sighed and cooed and dug her nails into his shoulders. He circled her breasts, placing tiny kisses on the very edge, where the swells just began, ignoring the nipples altogether. He was only half done when she lost her patience.

"Damn it, Cam," she reached for her nipples herself.

He grabbed her wrists. "Ah, ah ah. Put your hands over your head, missy."

"What?"

"Go on. Up over your head." His grin at her expression was, perhaps, a trifle evil.

"But—"

"But nothing. This is the Cam Jackson show. You are a canvas, and I'm painting on you. Come on. Do it."

With a gusty sigh, she raised her arms.

"Good girl. Leave them there."

"Get back to work. And quit driving me crazy."

"I want you crazy." To prove his point, he went back to work, making sure to go as slow as he could bear. Before long she was twitching restlessly.

As enjoyable as this torment was, he wanted, needed to continue his journey. Every inch of her was a new delight to relish. He made his way over her torso, appreciating the way the rise of her ribcage plunged to a flat belly. He spent a while exploring that creamy expanse before he suckled the rim of her bellybutton and dabbed in his tongue.

She quivered when he shifted downward. Sucked in a breath, held it, as he neared her haven. He loved that her thighs stole apart as he drew closer. That she wailed when he passed on by in favor of sampling the delicious skin of her thigh, the sensitive spot behind her knee and the ticklish arch of her graceful foot.

He would have spent more time on her toes, but even as she was steeped in anticipation, so was he.

He made his way up the other leg, although this trip was much quicker than the downward journey. He'd lost patience for this teasing game. He wanted to taste her and he wanted it bad.

She whimpered a little when he finally reached the crux of her thighs. He reverently opened her with his thumbs and stared at her beautiful hidden pearl. Then blew. Just blew. One slow, tender exhalation. Her body seized. Even as he watched, a glistening of cream seeped from her. He shuddered at the knowledge she was ready.

But she wasn't ready enough.

He drew a finger along her slit, intending to make his way to her hard, tight clit. But her heat, her slickness stayed his hand. He glanced up at her, lust searing him.

"What?" she whispered. "What's wrong?"

"You're so wet."

"Of course I'm wet. You've been teasing me for hours."

"Not hours."

"It feels like hours."

"I haven't even done the back."

She shot up on her elbows and glared at him. "You're not doing the back." And then, "At least not tonight. Come on. Finish it." She put her palm to his head and tried to push him down, down into her simmering nest.

He pushed back. "Did I say you could move your arms?"

"What?"

"Go on. Lay back down. Arms over your head. Let me do my thing."

"But—"

"You don't want me to tie them up there, do you?"

Her eyes widened and she nibbled her lower lip as she considered his threat. And then she said something that sent lust snaking through him. "Not tonight." She plopped back down and lifted her arms again, spreading her thighs wider. "Okay. Continue."

He loved the tremor in her voice.

She was on the edge, but he was right there with her. He didn't make her wait any longer. He lowered his head and drew his tongue lightly along her cleft. Her scent, her taste, sank in, grabbing him with vicious claws. He delved deeper, teasing the opening with his tongue, drinking her in. His nose nudged her clit and she flinched, groaned.

Poor thing. It really needed his attention.

So he returned, tasting his way to the crux of her vulva where that aching bundle of nerves awaited. He circled it, glorying in her response, her cries, the impatient thrusts of her hips. When he took her between his lips and sucked, she screamed, though it was muffled. He suspected if he looked up, he would see she'd draped her arm over her mouth to hold in the sound.

But he wasn't looking up. No way. No how.

He was too engrossed. Too fascinated by his discoveries. Too busy

She was crazy about him. Something, much like elation, curled in his gut. "Um, what do you mean?"

"The whole time I was plying her with my seductive whiles, she was talking about you. Cam this. Cam that. It's always been Cam for me."

"Always been... What?"

"Kind of off-putting. Also, she kisses like a cold fish."

The hell she did!

Holt grimaced. "Nothing. Not a hint of passion. No tongue, hell, no response at all. I must be losing my touch," he muttered.

Relief, twined with the trails of aggravation, seeped into Cam's soul. "Good." Fucking good. Fucking great.

"So..." Holt studied him from beneath thick, dark lashes. "Is it serious between you, or just a fling? Because if it's just a fling, if she's just fucking you to get it out of her system, I'd like to know."

Okay. He was going to have to murder his best friend. Awesome.

Holt winced at his expression. "Whoa. Chillaxe, Cam. I was just kidding."

"Were you? Were you really?"

"Quit snarling." Holt glanced up at the deck and paled. "They're watching us."

"Who?" Cam spun around and froze. Kristi stood on the deck gazing down at them with Bella and Cassie by her side.

"Don't want them to see us fight, now do you?"

Cam snorted. "They might find it entertaining to watch me beat your ass."

"Like you could beat my ass."

"I could."

"In your dreams."

They both laughed. They knew they were evenly matched.

"I don't know why you're even interested in Kristi. She's not your type." Cam grabbed his axe and headed for the tool shed.

Holt fell in beside him. "She's gorgeous."

"But not your *type*."

"Why do you say it like that?"

Cam raised a brow. "We all know about that club you go to in SoDo. You like submissive women who do what they're told." Definitely not Kristi. She never did what anyone told her.

"Ah, but sometimes it's more fun when they're disobedient."

"Regardless, it takes a certain kind of woman to go for that."

Holt shrugged. "I got a vibe from her. I thought...maybe..."

Cam gaped at him. "You got a *vibe* from her? *That* vibe?"

"A little bit. Yeah."

Holy shit. "Really?"

"You should try spanking her sometime. See what happens."

Cam boggled.

"Just sayin', dude. Just sayin'. Sometimes a little playful paddling can really heat up the bedroom."

Cam shook his head. "If I tried that, she'd have me drawn and quartered."

"Well, you'll never know unless you give it a shot."

Cam fit the axe into its holder, tossed his gloves onto the shelf and closed the shed, but his mind was in a whirl. He really wasn't into hardcore kink, but the thought of Kristi with her hands tied, or her lush body draped over his lap was…intriguing.

He glanced up at the deck. She sent him a smile and a wave.

Hmm. Maybe they should chat about it.

The idea had merit.

CHAPTER SIX

Everyone converged on the great room for lunch. It was hard getting Kristi alone with so many people milling around, but when the others were bumping into each other in the kitchen, whipping up some tacos, he caught her in the pantry.

He didn't bother with small talk. He just pulled her into his arms and kissed her.

"God, I missed you," he whispered, when they were both breathless and trembling. "Where'd you go last night?"

"I had to get back before, well, before they woke up."

All of a sudden, her obsession with keeping their relationship from the others stuck in his craw. He wasn't sure why. Maybe because Holt had kissed her. Maybe because he knew Andrew liked her too. Maybe because he just wanted them all to know she was taken.

The certainty of that resolution curled in his gut.

"We should just tell them. Then you can stay as long as you want tonight. All night." He dipped his head to kiss her again but he missed. She'd ducked away. Shock rippled through his system.

And then he got a glimpse of her face. His blood went cold at her expression.

"What? What is it?"

She stepped back and twined her fingers, not meeting his eyes.

He wasn't gonna like this. Not in the least.

"I-I just think maybe we should...cool it?"

Something within him howled. His gut clenched into a tight ball and acid tickled at the back of his throat. Heat—maybe anger—prickled his nape. He thought about stepping closer, boxing her in, kissing her again, but instead he took a step back. "You, ah, didn't enjoy it?" How he got those words out, he couldn't fathom. His tongue was like a stone.

Her gaze snapped to him, wide and surprised. "Didn't like it? Hell, Cam.

I loved it." Relief gushed. But then she frowned. "Did-didn't you like it?"

"Best fucking night of my life. I'd like to top it tonight. Right now. Why don't we, I dunno, go for a walk?" He didn't fancy fucking in the woods, but hell, he needed her again. And the squirrels probably wouldn't mind.

She shook her head. His mood would have plunged again, but she stepped closer and put her palm on his chest. Her scent curled around him. His pulse kicked up a notch. His body remembered how she'd felt coming to bliss around him. Mr. Happy awoke. With a vengeance. He shot up to full length in a heartbeat.

Softly, she said, "We can't. We shouldn't."

"What?" *Why the fuck not?* "Kristi, you better tell me what's going on."

"It's Bella."

Bella? What the hell did her sister have to do with this? He shook his head, unable to form the question.

"Did you know she has a thing for you? I didn't either. I was stunned. She knows what's going on between the two of us and she's really upset. I-I just couldn't do that to her. Not after..." She sighed.

"After what?"

Kristi nibbled her lip. "There was this guy in high school she was dating. He dumped her. For me."

"And you dated him?"

She shrugged. "I know it was wrong. But I was a stupid kid. I was flattered by the attention. He eventually dumped me for someone else, but by then it didn't matter. The damage was done. I don't ever think she forgave me. It was years before she would even talk to me again. Cam—I can't do that to her. Not again. I can't."

"This is different."

"Not really."

"I'm not dating Bella. I'm not interested in dating Bella. Even if there was no you and me, I wouldn't be dating Bella." He did it then. Cornered her. Maybe Holt had it right. Maybe the way to manage a woman was to dominate her. So he backed her up against the shelves of canned goods and took her mouth in a punishing kiss.

She resisted, but not for long. Then she wrapped her arms around his neck and gave as good as she got. Her response enflamed him. He reached down and lifted her leg, wrapping it around his waist, giving him access to her crotch. He rubbed her there, in that tender spot, through her jeans as he fucked her mouth. With his other hand, he held her chin still so he could take what he wanted.

A can of soup fell to the floor. And another. Cam ignored them. He fiddled with the buttons of her jeans.

She broke away, gasping. "Cam. Not here. They'll hear."

"Let them fucking hear."

"Oh, they can hear." A deep, amused voice floated into the room. Cam whipped around to see Holt leaning on the doorjamb. Smirking. "It sounds like you're wrestling with a walrus in here."

"God." Kristi buried her face in his chest.

"Don't worry, Kris," Holt chirped. "They don't know what you two are up to. They sent me to find out what the ruckus was." He glanced at Cam. "But really? In the pantry?"

"It *was* private."

"Apparently not private enough. Come along you two. Let's join the others. And do try to behave." He leaned closer and hissed, "Try not to fuck on the table while we're eating."

Kristi smacked his shoulder as she passed, quickly ducking from the room, her cheeks ablaze.

And thank God. Because if she hadn't hit Holt, Cam was going to for sure.

It bugged him that Kristi deliberately took the seat across and down the table from him at lunch. He'd had it in mind to toy with her the way he had the night before. Hell, she wouldn't even meet his eye. So he focused on Bella instead.

He'd never had the sense that Bella had a thing for him. In all the years he'd known her, she'd never flirted with him. And she didn't clam up around him, the way some women did when they had a crush. If there was anyone around the table Bella wasn't paying any attention to—like at all—it was Holt. She didn't so much as crack a smile at his jokes.

The whole thing baffled him, but he was determined to figure it out. He couldn't let this thing with Kristi just…end. Not before it even really started. The very thought gave him cold chills. He'd wanted her, dreamed about her, fantasized about her for so long, but that had been nothing compared to the reality. And now, now that he'd had her, he wasn't letting her go. He couldn't.

Drew reached across in front of him grabbing another taco from the platter, interrupting his gloomy reverie. "So Kristi," he said, shoveling some chips into his mouth, "how's everything in the shop?"

Kristi glanced up. Her gaze, on its way to Andrew, clashed with Cam's. He took the opportunity to send her a speaking look. It said: *I want you.* She got the message. A blush crept up her cheeks. "It's, um, fine."

"And Lucy? How's she doing? I hardly ever see the two of you anymore."

Holt grinned. "Why isn't she here this weekend too?" Holt was an evil bastard. He knew damned well why. This was Lane's weekend. After that last blow up, he and Lucy had agreed to share the house the way other couples shared their kids. One weekend at a time. Always separate. It was better for everyone.

Kristi took a sip of her water. "One of us has to stay at the store. Besides, she has a date tonight."

It was comical the way Lane's head snapped up at that. The clack of his teeth was audible. He swore beneath his breath. A muscle in his cheek bunched. "A date? What kind of date?"

"Oh, you know." Kristi shrugged. "The kind of date where a nice, successful guy with an awesome job picks you up at seven and takes you out for a romantic dinner. Maybe a little dancing. A walk on the beach. And then afterwards…" She fluttered her lashes. "Well, you know what happens afterwards."

Yeah, Kristi could be a little evil too.

Lane hopped up, stormed to the fridge and pulled out a beer. He popped it open, took a long draw and wiped his mouth on his sleeve. "So who is this nice successful guy with an awesome job?" Holy shit. Was that really a snarl? From laidback, easygoing Lane?

"A customer. Pretty cute too."

"Cute?" Cassie leaned forward. "Do tell."

"You know. Tall. Dark. Supremely good-looking." Kristi sighed hugely, focusing all her attention on Lane.

Cam bit back his snicker. Definitely evil.

Lane grimaced. "Is it serious?"

Kristi sighed. "Lane. It's a date. It's dinner. I didn't mean to infer anything more was—"

"Maybe I should stop by. Check this dude out. Who knows what his real motives are."

"Dating a scorching hot chick with bags of cash?" This from Drew. His smirk wilted in the face of Lane's fierce glower.

"Are you saying my ex is a hot chick?" A growl.

"She's beautiful." Cassie said in a soothing voice. She set her hand on Lane's arm. "Calm down. You and Lucy are divorced. It's been over a year. It's only natural for the two of you to start dating again."

Holt grinned. "And aren't you seeing that… What's her name?" He snapped his fingers several times. "Chesty McChesterson?"

"Delilah." Lane crossed his arms over his chest.

"Right. Delilah. No man tapping that well has a right to complain he's thirsty."

A laugh bubbled in Cam's throat. "Tapping that well?"

Holt shrugged. "What can I say? When I think of Delilah's boobs, I just wax poetic-like."

Drew's gray eyes took on a mischievous light. "She is blessed."

"Oh, right," Bella wrinkled her nose. "As if *those* were a gift from God."

CHAPTER SEVEN

After lunch they went down to the beach and the girls hunted for driftwood while Holt and Cam pulled the kayaks out of the boathouse. It was a beautiful spring day, but still far too cold to go swimming. Drew joined them, grumbling about being left with the mess.

Holt turned to Cam as he handed out the life vests. "You coming?"

Cam's gaze swung to the dock where Bella sat, soaking in the rare shafts of sun, reading a book. "Nah. I think I'll just hang out." Kristi shot him a frown and he quirked a brow in response. She looked adorable with the orange vest nudging her chin, but he was bound and determined to talk to her sister, no matter how nervous *she* was about it. "You all have fun. I think the whales are out."

Cassie nodded, "We saw one this morning. I wish I brought my camera."

They all piled in the kayaks—Holt and Kristi in one and Cassie and Drew in the other—and even though Holt and Kristi were in the same boat, Cam didn't care. He had business to take care of and this would probably be his only opportunity to get Bella alone. He watched as they paddled past the gentle surf into the open water. Drawing in a deep breath, he turned and headed for the dock.

It was a floater, anchored to the shore by pylons sunk into the sand. It swayed a little as he walked to where Bella sat at the end. She glanced up as he took the lounge chair next to her. But he didn't lounge. He perched on the side, and studied her until her face puckered up.

"What?"

"Can we talk?"

She dropped her book onto her chest. "Sure."

Crap. He should have planned this better. He didn't know what to say. He decided to just dive in. "I was just wondering how long?"

She shook her head. "How long? How long what?"

"How long have you had a thing for me?"

Her mouth fell open. She gaped at him. "Wh-what?"

"You know. How long have you had this crush on me?"

She sat up then, facing him, knee to knee. "What makes you think I have a crush on you?"

"You don't?"

Her snort was a dead giveaway. That and her laugh.

Really? Was the prospect so hilarious?

"Cam Jackson, you are so full of yourself."

He put out a lip. "I am not. It's just, Kristi said—"

"Kristi said what? What? What did Kristi say?"

"You know." He raked his fingers through his hair all the way to his nape.

"Uh, no. I don't know."

"She said we couldn't…"

"Couldn't what?"

"Continue." There. Surely that was clear enough.

"Continue?" Hell. Apparently not. "Continue what?"

"Our…" He made a motion that should have been more than illustrative. She blinked. Like an owl. "You know. Our thing. Because you had these feelings and she didn't want to hurt you."

Why this annoyed Bella, Cam had no clue. "Are you serious?" She leaped to her feet and stormed to the edge of the dock and stared out at the kayaks in the distance. "She told you?" And then she spun around. "Wait. She said she couldn't continue her thing with you…or her thing with Holt?"

Now he bounced up. "She doesn't have a thing with Holt." At least she'd better not. "Did she say she had a thing with Holt?" Unease trickled through him. Kristi told him there was nothing. She'd *convinced* him there was nothing. Had she been telling the truth, or just playing him? No. He couldn't bear that thought—

"I saw them kissing last night."

Oh. *That.* His tension released.

"I saw them, Cam." Bitterness bubbled in her voice. "Why does it always work out like that? Why do they always fall for her? Am I not pretty?"

Aw, shit. Tears. He hated tears.

"You're very pretty. Really Bella, any guy would be lucky to have you." Based on her expression, she wasn't buying it. He decided to get to the point. "What you saw last night? It's not what you think it was."

"My sister? In a passionate embrace with the man I—with a man?" She crossed her arms over her chest and scowled at him. "What else could it be?" Bella froze. "Wait… You said she didn't want to continue this affair with you because I had a thing for you? Is she fucking you both?" she asked gloomily.

"No." In fact, hell to the no. "It's Kristi and me. Not Holt. At all. Like even a little bit. Not ever. Never." He emphasized this point with a slash of his hand and then added a couple more "evers" just for good measure.

"She's having an affair with you?" She narrowed her eyes. "Are you— are you sure?"

"Yup. Pretty sure." Pretty damn fucking sure.

"So you're the one she was with all last night?"

"All night long." Holt probably spent the night in his room nursing a bruised jaw. "He did kiss her, but only to test the waters. She told him to get lost." Or at least, something like that.

"So…it's you and Kristi?"

"Yep."

"Oh." Her expression cleared. "Well. That's okay then." She shot him a perky grin and plopped back down in her lounger and picked up her book.

But they weren't done. Not by a long shot. He shifted her legs over and sat at her side. She frowned.

"So I have your blessing?"

"My what?"

"Your blessing. To date your sister. Because it's important to her. And Bella, I really care—I mean, I really, really care."

"Mercy." She sighed and patted his cheek. "You are kind of adorable, I suppose. Yes. You have my blessing." But then her smile morphed into another fierce glower. The tiny diamond in her nose winked. "But I swear unto God in heaven above, if you so much as breathe a hint about my feelings for Holt to anyone—*anyone*—I'll have your guts for garters. Do you hear me?"

"Yes ma'am."

"Well, okay then. Get off my chair."

He did. He sat on the end of his lounger with his elbows on his knees and his fingers linked, and stared out at the tiny kayaks bobbing in the water in the distance trying to tame the elation rioting in his gut.

The road was clear. Kristi was his. Tonight, he'd have her again. And the night after that. And, hopefully, all the nights after that.

Little did she know it, but Bella was going to be his sister-in-law some day. Hopefully someday soon.

"So," he said as a gentle breeze lifted his hair. He closed his eyes and turned his face up to the sun. "What's the deal with you and Holt?"

He chuckled when her book hit his back.

* * * * *

The kayak scraped the shore and Kristi sighed. "That was great."

"It was." Holt's voice rumbled behind her. Something in the timbre of his voice snagged her attention and she glanced back. He was glaring at the dock. She swung around to follow his gaze and saw Cam and Bella hugging. It was a quick hug, nothing that should cause those shards of jealousy to stab her belly. But then he kissed her. Only her cheek. But still…

Fury snarled in her breast.

"What the hell is that all about?" Holt grumbled. He hopped out of the boat into the water with no care for his expensive boots. Kristi stood, but plopped down again when he yanked the boat further onto the shore, his attention trained on the dock.

"She has a thing for him, I guess."

His head whipped around. "She does?"

"I guess."

Belatedly, he thrust out his hand and helped her from the boat. "I thought you and he…"

"So did I." She collected their life vests and paddles. "I'm going to put these away and then have a chat with him. Can you and Drew get the boats?"

But Holt wasn't paying attention. He was staring at the dock, scrubbing his chin with his palm.

Cam found her in the boathouse hanging up the life vests. "Hey you. How was your trip?"

She didn't look at him. "Fine."

"See any whales?"

"Not today."

"Bummer." Silence crackled. He broke it. "I, uh, had a chat with Bella."

"I noticed."

"Did you?" Why was there amusement threading through his tone? She turned to glare at him. Yup. A big old smile plastered on his handsome face.

"I saw you hugging her."

"Why wouldn't I hug her? She's my friend. Your sister and…we worked everything out." Clearly he was pleased with himself.

"You worked it all out?"

"Yep. Apparently it was just a misunderstanding. I'm not the dude she has a thing for."

Her brow rumpled. "You're not? Who is?"

"I can't say."

50

minutes ago?"

"A few minutes ago I was…hungry."

He stood and fastened his jeans and pulled her close to his side, where she belonged. "And now you're sated?"

"Not quite."

He frowned at her. "Not quite?"

"Nope." She shot him a impish look. "Now I want a margarita." They headed toward the stairs together, arms linked. "Later," she said. "Later you can sate me."

Yeah. He would. And then some.

CHAPTER NINE

When they came through the slider, Cassie already had the blender going. She had a secret recipe for knock-you-naked margaritas, which were absolutely divine. Bella and Kristi joined her in the kitchen to whip up some nachos while the guys all clomped down to the basement to watch the Mariners. As far as Kristi could tell, Lane was still in his room.

"Maybe we should check on him." She glanced at his door.

Cassie shook her head. "I'm sure he's fine. No doubt he'll come out when he smells the food." But he didn't. The guys surfaced from the basement, though. Apparently the game had been lame. They all swarmed around the table and sucked down margaritas and inhaled nachos, laughing and joking and brutally teasing Drew about his new tattoo.

Bella started it all when he pulled up his shirtsleeve to show it—and his bulging biceps—off. She snorted.

Drew frowned at her. "What?"

Bella shrugged. "I didn't think firemen were allowed to get tattoos."

Drew made a face. "We're firemen. Not slaves."

"Civil servants," Holt muttered. "Close enough."

"I can't believe you got a puppy." Bella grinned. "Of all the tattoos in all the world. You got a puppy."

"I like dogs."

Bella ignored him. "Not a bulldog or a Rottweiler or a pit bull. A puppy."

"It's a Dalmatian. I'm a fireman. It makes sense."

Cassie leaned closer. "I think it's cute."

"Me too." Holt smirked. "C'mon baby, come to papa, I'll kiss your fuckin' Dalmatian."

This, of course, was followed by a chorus of "Come out to the cooooast, we'll get togeeeether, have a few laaaaughs..." because none of them could resist. Movie quotes were kind of a thing with them. They loved watching the classics over and over again, competing to see who remembered the most lines. They loved it almost as much as they all loved football.

But not quite as much.

Because, after all… Football.

A knock at the back door surprised them. The neighbors rarely visited.

Cassie was closest, so she hopped up to answer it. Lane opened his door as she passed. He looked like hell with red eyes and hair all matted to his head. There was a pillow streak on his cheek.

Kristi heard the rumble of voices but couldn't make out any words, but then her belly lurched. She knew who it was.

She leaped to her feet as Rolf pushed past Cassie and Lane. His gaze rounded the room and settled on her. Every man around the table rose as well. When Rolf stepped closer, they all bristled. His intense expression morphed into that charming mien she'd once found so irresistible. "There you are, baby. I've been hunting all over for you."

"Here I am." It was funny how her body reacted to him, especially now. There was no excitement. No thrill at the sight of him—not like she felt with Cam. Only a vague unease.

In the beginning, she'd thought his moodiness sexy, but it had gotten old quick. And though they'd been together for three years, the magic had evaporated long ago. Kristi didn't know why they'd stayed together. Probably just habit.

A bad reason to remain in a relationship with someone you didn't love to the depth of your being.

Rolf stepped closer. His voice dropped an octave. "Kristi. We need to talk."

"There's nothing to talk about."

"Yes. There is. Please. Five minutes." He glared around the room again. "In private."

In private? No way. She waved toward the deck. "Outside."

"Okay."

She led the way through the slider and turned to face him.

He closed the door. "Kristi. Honey. It wasn't what it looked like."

She crossed her arms over her chest. "Really? It looked like your white ass going to town on Savannah."

"Okay. I screwed up. It won't happen again."

Wouldn't it? She wasn't so sure. "Has it ever happened before?"

"What?" The flicker of guilt in his eyes was a dead giveaway.

"How many women, Rolf? How many women have you screwed since we've been together?"

He shrugged. "Not that many."

"Not that many?" Mortification washed through her. She'd been a fool to stay with him. To be with him.

A red tide rose on his cheeks. "None. None, baby." And at her glower, "Okay. Just the one. Just that one time."

"Right."

"Come on, Kristi. Give me another chance."

Certainty, unlike any certainty she'd ever known, settled in her gut. "It's over Rolf."

"Sweetheart..." He stepped closer and made a move to pull her into his arms. She evaded him.

A movement to her left, through the wall of windows, caught her attention. She glanced over to see Lane, Drew, Holt and Cam standing, in formation, tracking Rolf's every move, like ancient warriors surveying the field of a coming battle.

Love swelled in her chest. For all of them. One in particular. They would always be there for her. Always keep her safe. Her Dawgs.

Rolf followed her gaze and frowned. "I've always hated those guys."

She shook her head. "Don't you see? That's the problem here. Not Savannah...or any other woman. We simply aren't a good fit." Hardly a new revelation. For her at least.

Rolf gaped at her. "What are you talking about? We're perfect together."

"No. We aren't." Not even close. For one thing, he didn't like any of her friends. And he didn't like *football*. She should have known...

"Aw, come on, baby. Don't be like this." His voice took on a wheedling quality. He tipped his head to the side and sent her a cajoling smile. "We can work it out."

"There's nothing to work out, Rolf. I'm sorry. It's over."

He scratched his head and blew out a sigh. "Okay. Listen. I've been thinking. Maybe it's time to take our relationship to the next level."

"The next—what?"

"You know. I want you to move in with me."

This he said, just as the slider opened. So those were the words Cam heard.

"The fuck she will!" he bellowed.

A tiny glow lit in her chest. She liked the way his fury felt. At least, about this.

Rolf's cajoling expression morphed into a sneer. He propped his hands on his hips and gave Cam an insolent once-over. "Fuck off, douche wad. This isn't any of your business."

"The hell it's not. She's not moving in with you. She's moving in with me."

"I am?" Oh. This was news to her.

Cam winced and shot her an apologetic grin. "I was going to ask you in a week or so. Maybe after our third date."

"We're having a third date?"

"It's on the schedule."

"The schedule?"

A flush crawled up his cheeks. "The schedule in my head. I have it all worked out. I told you I've been thinking about you for a while."

Rolf went ape-shit. "What. The. Fuck," he snarled. Have you been making moves on my girl all this time?" He poked Cam's chest with a belligerent finger.

Stupid move. It brought him back to Cam's attention. That sweet, adorable face went all Highlander.

"She's not your girl," he snapped. "She's mine."

"Since when?" Rolf shoved Cam's shoulder. He wheeled on Kristi. "Are you fucking him, you whore?"

Uh oh.

Dumb.

Dumb de dumb dumb.

Before she could say a word to defend herself—as though she would even bother—Cam's fist smashed into Rolf's cheek and he went reeling. He collapsed against the railing and slumped onto the deck.

"Dude," Holt said from the door, "you're gonna have to stop hitting people."

Cam shook out his hand and shot his friend a dark look. "I only hit them when they really need hitting."

"Yeah." Holt cleared his throat. "I'll remember that." With a glance at Rolf, he stepped back inside and slid the door shut.

Cam pulled Kristi into his arms. "Are you okay?"

"I'm fine," she laughed. She was better than okay. "But what about you?" She kissed his knuckles. "That had to hurt."

"It hurt so good." He glowered at Rolf and Rolf's eyes widened. He skittered out of reach like a crab and then leaped to his feet and escaped around the corner of the house.

No one was following.

Because finally, they were alone.

Kristi grinned and turned her attention back to Cam. "Did you mean what you said?"

"About what?"

"About a future? For us?"

"Shit, Kristi. Of course I meant it. Didn't I make myself clear last night?"

"Not really. We agreed on rebound."

"That was just a ploy!"

"A what?"

He cringed at her screech. "You know. A ploy? To get you in bed?"

She smacked his shoulder. "You. Did. Not."

"Kinda."

His expression was sheepish. And adorable. And she loved it.

"I'm serious about dating you, Kristi. Really dating. And when you're ready we can move in together and..."

"And?"

"More. If, you know, we both want more."

She had a suspicion she would want more. "I'd like that."

"Would you?"

"Definitely."

He stared at her for a long moment. "Holt said something that intrigued me."

"Forget about Holt."

He chuckled. "I can't forget about this."

"All right." She looped her arms around his neck and leaned against him. "What did Holt say that was so intriguing?"

"He said a spanking can really spice up a sex life."

"Umm hmm," she said. "Sounds like Holt."

"Well. What do you think? Is that something you...might be interested in?"

She focused on the hairs erupting in the vee of his shirt. Stroked them with a fingertip. "I dunno. Maybe."

"Maybe?"

"If *you're* interested."

"Oh, I am. At least I think I am. We could, you know, explore. I bet Bella's store has some interesting stuff we could play with."

"Right. Like I want to do my sex shopping at my sister's boutique?"

He leaned in and kissed her. "We'll go by when she's not there. Okay?"

"Okay."

"And that spanking?" Damn, he was insistent. "Are you up for it tonight?"

"Tonight? Really?"

"Umm hmm." He silenced her with a long, leisurely kiss.

When he pulled away she was breathless. "Okay, Mr. Jackson. You've convinced me. We'll try a little spanking tonight." She shot him a fiendish grin. "But I sure hope your ass can take it."

The look on his face was priceless.

BOOKS BY SABRINA YORK

Adam's Obsession (Erotic Contemporary, Ellora's Cave)
Dark Duke (Erotic Regency, Ellora's Cave)
Brigand (Erotic Regency, Ellora's Cave)
Dark Fancy (Erotic Regency, Ellora's Cave)
Devlin's Dare: A Tryst Island Erotic Romance (Erotic Contemporary)
Dragonfly Kisses: A Tryst Island Erotic Romance (Erotic
Contemporary)
Extreme Couponing (Erotic Contemporary, Ellora's Cave)
Fierce (One Night Stand, Decadent Press)
Five Alarm Fire (Erotic Contemporary for the High Octane Heroes
Anthology, Cleis Press)
Folly (Erotic Regency, Ellora's Cave)
Heart of Ash: A Tryst Island Erotic Romance (Erotic Contemporary)
Lust Eternal (Erotic Fantasy, Ellora's Cave)
Pushing Her Buttons (Erotic Contemporary, Ellora's Cave)
Making Over Maris (Erotic Contemporary, Ellora's Cave)
Man Hungry (Erotic Contemporary, Ellora's Cave)
Rebound: A Tryst Island Erotic Romance (Erotic Contemporary)
Rising Green (Erotic Horror, Ellora's Cave)
Saving Charlotte (Erotic Contemporary for the
Smokin' Hot Firemen Anthology, Cleis Press)
Smoking Holt: A Tryst Island Erotic Romance (Erotic Contemporary)
Training Tess (Erotic Contemporary, Ellora's Cave)
Trickery (Erotic Contemporary with Magical Elements, Ellora's Cave)
Tristan's Temptation (Erotic Contemporary, Ellora's Cave)

CPSIA information can be obtained
at www.ICGtesting.com
Printed in the USA
LVHW082141200222
711589LV00032B/1063